T0082595

CAUGHT BETWEEN THE BLOOD AND THE FIRE

Yolanda Grady

authorHOUSE®

AuthorHouse™
1663 Liberty Drive
Bloomington, IN 47403
www.authorhouse.com
Phone: 1 (800) 839-8640

Published by AuthorHouse 09/30/2017

ISBN: 978-1-5462-1023-8 (sc)
ISBN: 978-1-5462-1022-1 (e)

Library of Congress Control Number: 2017914817

Print information available on the last page.

Contents

Introduction

Torn Between Heaven and Hell

I'm screaming "get your damn hands off me! I didn't do nothing!"

I punched that red neck motherfucker in the back of his neck. The next thing I know, the police officer hit me in the head and on the ground I went. When I came around to see where I was, the pain hit me. I felt like the whole dame police department was standing on my back. I remember being tied up and put in the police car. Blood was dripping from my mouth while my hands and feet were bound in handcuffs. I am laying on this hard bunk bed in a cold cell block, asking myself "what in the hell did I do to get myself in jail?"

I'm screaming to the guard "let my ass out, I am a nurse! I got to go to work! This bullshit is not right! You beat my ass then locked me up. I haven't done shit to nobody where is my motherfucking lawyer, bitch?"

The guard came up to my cell and said "if you don't shut up you will be put in confinement and nobody will hear your black ass, bitch! I will leave your dumb ass to die! You're a drunk slut, take a seat! Have I made myself clear?"

I looked at her and knew this guard was not the typical kind of jail guard; she would make my life miserable.

"God," I began to pray, "I have always been able to hear your voice even when I don't obey. Talk to me now and tell me what to do." I turned around and walked back to my bunk with my head down. "I got to get out of this hell hole," I thought to myself, "before one of us gets hurt and it just might be me." I began to pray again; "God, I don't hear you anymore.

God, it is Trina. I made my bed in HELL again! God, you said you would be here with me."

Laying on this steel has me thinking about my senseless fucked up life. Who would have thought that the pastor's wife would be behind bars? My pimp ass husband! The preacher decided to sleep with our daughter's best friend, who just so happens to be my niece. I wish I could kill that man a second time but what's done is done. I am not even in jail for killing my husband. The police locked me up because my dead husband's eighteen-year-old baby's mama had the nerve to leave her baby on my doorsteps.

•••••••••••●○○○○○○○○○○

Let me back up to the beginning and introduce myself. I have spent the last thirty-five years struggling in a jungle of a community where poverty is at its maximum high. My family drama has set me up to spend more quality time in Peppermint County Jail. This time, my fifth time, things are different; I am First Lady T of the church. I need to get the hell out of here. I have a flock to attend to. I screamed again, release me now!

Chapter 1

REJECTION - WHO'S YOUR MOTHER?

My birth name is Trina Michelle Right. I was born November 22, 1981 to the unknown. My mother was a black woman that was known as the neighborhood whore and my father was a dope pusher that became her pimp. My father was biracial and had many women in his life. When my mother got pregnant she became his main lady. However, when I was born, my father decided that my mother should give me up for adoption because having a child to care for would slow down his business. My mother gave me up to the state but my father's sister adopted me. It was only after I was raped by a family member that my adoptive mother revealed to me the truth; what I had grown up thinking were my mother and father were in fact my Aunt and Uncle.

I have many fond memories from my childhood but I first noticed that my life was far from perfect when "Uncle" Mike started hanging around all the time. My eyes as a child became open to so many of life's challenges. My parents, Mr. Mark and Mrs. Ruth Right, had a loving relationship as far as I could see. They were very known and respected in our community; a ghetto dubbed "Pigsville". Helping me along the way was my older brother Clyde. He was ten years older than me and he was the greatest brother I could have ever hoped for. Whenever I was hungry, he would make sure that I got a bowl of Apple Jacks. Our dad would take us fishing with him all the time until Clyde was old enough to take care of me. My dad was on disability while mom worked two jobs. My dad had served in the army before my time and mom said he just was not the same afterwards. I was five years old when Clyde became my unofficial babysitter. Clyde did not have a lot of friends aside from a few cousins and some neighborhood boys. My dad's brother, Uncle Mike, had two sons, Nash and Garret, who were close with Clyde. In the neighborhood, Freddy and Big Ham were Clyde's best friends. They looked like brothers but they were first cousins.

Every weekend Clyde crew got together with him. Everybody in the neighborhood knew them as "Boys in the Hood." My parents had a finished basement that served as a clubhouse of sorts for the "Boys in the Hood". After school, they would congregate there to spin the latest rap records and host their own impromptu rap battles. But somehow, their rap battles would always turn into a game of craps. Luckily for them, our dad didn't care. Our mom, however, was a little more involved; whenever she would clean the basement, she would find evidence of their little dice games. She was no fool and made it very clear to them.

As for me, my three closest friends growing up were Cree, Lacy, and Bella. We also started kindergarten together and remained friends until my life began to unravel later on. Bella was the younger sister of Clyde's friend Freddy. Freddy would walk us to school every day. Freddy would take us to the candy store by their house and let us get whatever we wanted. Freddy would call me Little Redbone. I would reply "That's not my name! It's Trina!"

Freddy would fire back "okay, Little Redbone." I would shake my head and giggle because Freddy was so funny.

Sunday was very important to my mom. There was always a big dinner with family and friends. I loved spending time with everyone. Those were the fun times growing up in the hood.

I wanted to be married just like my mother and father but I wanted a big house and have six children. But my whole life changed when my Uncle Mike started coming over drinking with my daddy. Sometimes he would spend the night because he claimed to be too drunk to drive. He would always bring me candy and chips and sometimes he would take me to the store with him and I would get to pick out anything I want. I really loved my Uncle Mike he was the best uncle ever. One day, my brother and cousins had got in some big trouble. I did not understand when my brother went away at seventeen. Mom told me that Clyde was going away for sixty-five years and that was all that she ever said on the matter. My brother's friends still walked me to school but I had lost my favorite brother and my babysitter.

One day, I remember mom calling out to dad and asking, "Mark are you going fishing today? I got to do a double shift tonight. I won't be home to put Trina on the school bus."

My dad replied, "Yes Ruth! I'm going fishing. My brother Mike can babysit Trina while I'm gone."

The day my parents left me alone with Uncle Mike was the day my virginity was stolen. I was seven years old when Uncle Mike started giving me alcohol to relax me. He would do things to me that I did not like. He would say it is our little secret and that I shouldn't tell anyone.

One night, I overheard mom tell dad, "I don't want Mike taking care of Trina anymore. He can't take care of his own damn self! Mark, you better take care of your own daughter or go get a damn job! Fishing don't pay the bills."

When I heard this, I thought my problems were over. No more hide and seek with Uncle Mike. My mother never was home, she worked nonstop through the week. My dad was always "fishing". I found out that fish had a name; Wanda the Drunk. And, in the meantime, Uncle Mike had gone to jail for drinking and driving so I was safe again.

When I turned ten, my mother let me stay at home by myself while she worked herself to death. I can't blame her, my daddy stayed drunk with Ms. Wanda the fish that lived in the alley. When I turned thirteen my school friends were all hanging out, getting money, and wearing the fresh J's that I was dreaming of. I knew this school shit was not for me. Broke kids stay in school, rich ones chase the money. I joined a west side gang called "Put Your Hands Up". To be initiated all I had to do is rob somebody. I took my friends over to Uncle Mike house. I felt he owed me all his money. I was going to give all his jewelry to my man Chuck, so he could look good. We waited for his drunk ass to get home. We all had on ski masks to protect our identity but in my heart, I wanted him to see me. When Uncle Mike came home, he opened his door and walked into the doorway. We all put guns to his head and walked in with him. "Put your hands up!" we yelled. "Give me your money!" Chuck screamed.

Uncle Mike said he didn't have any money. My new squad beat his ass. We trashed his apartment took his eleven hundred dollars that I found under his mattress. We went through his drawers and found a couple of pounds of marijuana. I was so pissed off I hit that sorry ass molester in the head with my Tec-9. I wanted Uncle Mike ass to suffer for everything he did to me. We let him know if he called the police we would come back. Uncle Mike never put his nasty hands on me again. I made sure Uncle Mike knew it was me even though I wore a mask while everybody was destroying his place. I took a red marker and wrote on his sheets in big letters: TOUCH ME AGAIN AND YOU WILL DIE!

After that, Uncle Mike stopped coming around. I decided to tell my mother about her brother-in-law touching me. "Uncle Mike" was Michael Carl Right and was a deacon in the church. Who would think he would hurt little girls? I thought my mother would be devastated at the news. I found out none of these people were my blood family. Nobody knew where my biological mother and father were. Ruth was my aunt and Mark was nobody to me. Who in the hell would just lie about being your parents?! No more trying to rationalize with people that are temporary in my life.

One day, I waited until Ruth had left for work. I left her a note on the refrigerator saying, "I am moving out. Do not want to be contacted. Love, Trina, your niece".

How dare these overbearing people be my foster parents. They had destroyed my life by betraying me. They left me in the care of a drunk. Uncle Mike took my virginity then forced me to have sex with him for years.

I knew I had a real family in "PUT YOUR HANDS UP". I joined my friends that had it going on. They slept downtown under the bridge. It was not as bad as I thought to live on my own. It was cool to have my own place with no bills attached. Only struggle was food. My squad and I put our money together for whatever we needed. But I missed Ruth's Sunday meals. I could still smell that fried chicken and Mac and Cheese even when I was living under the bridge. Ruth thought I was not old enough to live this life on my own. If my parents would have told me my identity earlier in my life I could have protected myself. My pain would not have pierced my heart and left me lifeless on the dangerous streets of Pigsville. An investigation about my family history must take place. Too many lies have been told.

Chapter 2

Abandoned - Lost in the Trenches

A couple of years on the streets of Pigsville had left their mark on me. I had to grow up quick. Despite all the joy and love I had experienced in my early childhood, I couldn't help but feel like I had now been dealt a rotten hand. While I found some comfort in "Put Your Hands Up!", it was no replacement for the Right family. I really missed them all, even though I was still bitter about being deceived about my biological family. I was determined to seek out my birth parents. What gave them the right to give me away to the State of Indiana? While I was grateful that Ruth took me in as a baby, I was still angry that she had hidden the truth from me. Clyde, my brother, now my cousin, was no longer my savior. He had chosen a life of crime and the judge had decided his new home was the Peppermint Penitentiary Maximum Security Facility for sixty-five years.

I went to my old neighborhood Pigsville to chill with my homegirls; this was my safe place. I knew the love was real and nobody could change that. I told my best friend, Lacy, to go to the corner store and buy some Swishers. We were ready to get our smoke on. But when Lacy returned with the smokes, she came with a familiar face; Freddy. Once my brother's childhood friend, he was now the undisputed king of Pigsville. Now a grown man, Freddy was all muscles from head to toe. When I saw him there with Lacy, his muscles glistened with sweat in the summer heat. His multiple trips to jail had left his arms and chest covered with intricate tattoos. His body art gave him a sexual glow. He was what I was looking for in a man. Even though he had been my brother's best friend and I had been so young, I had always had a crush on him. Now Freddy was twenty-five years old, with four children from different mothers and long, black, dreadlocks twisted down his back.

My saying for Freddy was, "Papa was a rolling stone where ever he laid his hat was his home." Freddy got to talking to the girls and me and invited us to hang out with him and his crew at the club that night. I responded with a "yes!" so quickly that I couldn't help but laugh. "Little Redbone," he said, "you are going with me but I am still in charge of you," he joked. "I am going to babysit you tonight."

My girls were laughing. I was looking at him saying to myself he really need to stop smoking. I don't like your old ass. I kept smiling so he could take his ass home or anywhere. He was really making me mad, he smoked my blunt up. Freddy was very conceited and could get on my nerves, Freddy and I quickly reconnected and bonded on a deeper level than we had when we were kids. I knew I could get anything from Freddy because of his friendship to my brother. He would leave new clothes and shoes for me at his mother's house to pick up so that I always had something nice to wear. During that time, I frequently found myself grinning from ear to ear. He always had top-brand clothes for me, thanks to his ghetto booster connections. They rip off retail stores and sell the merchandise on the streets. They always hooked him up with top-brand clothes and shoes.

Eventually, Freddy's mom, Ms. Capri's house, became a refuge for my friends and me. We knew we could always go there if we needed to rest and relax. We would kick it with her until it was time to go out and party. Freddy always made sure we would eat and shower at his mother's house. She was so welcoming to us because she hated the idea of us running the streets.

That first night we ended up hanging out with Freddy and his friends; I was feeling excited despite my insecurities. My girls Lacy, Cree, and Savanna all came to party with us. They wore halter tops with cut up jeans, 6in heels, with multicolored gemstone accents. I, on the other hand, had developed some body complexes. I had always been the tallest girl in my class. My feet were so big (I wore a size twelve). When I was younger, I felt like so many of my features were masculine. I knew I had to look like my father. I had to keep my hair done. Sometimes I would be harassed and teased when I wore my brother's basketball clothes. I became a fighter at an early age. I was pestered all the time. But as I became a young woman, my body finally began to develop the way I wanted it to. I felt feminine for the first time. Men would go crazy over me when I would go out. But for tonight, I decided to play it safe; no heels for me. Even though I had a more feminine physique I was still 6ft tall. I didn't want to appear any taller than I already was. I decided to wear a long red halter dress with the back fully out that night, with black appealing diamond studded sandals with my toes out. I knew I was going to have to give Freddy some of my goodies that night. Even though I was only 15 at the time, I sensed chemistry with Freddy and I was excited at the thought of being with the king of Pigsville.

One day, Ms. Capri said "My son better rent you a storage unit! You are taking up too much space in my room, Trina. You better get your shit together! Go make up with your mother cuz you only get one!"

I looked at Ms. Capri with glazing eyes. "God must have thought I needed two that's why I am over here!"

I really liked my six outfits that Freddy had left for me: six Victoria Secrets panty and bra sets. I didn't need a bra or panties that night because the dress was banging all by itself. I guess he felt like he didn't need to get me shoes. I had plenty of shoes to choose from in Ms. Capri's closet. Freddy knew that his mother and I shared a love of shoes. That night I carried my silver clutch purse with my MAC lip gloss, MAC Foundation, fifty-dollar bill, and Smith & Wesson 9mm pink pistol, ready for whatever the night had in store for me. Despite the safety and care I had experienced as a young girl, my experiences with Uncle Mike and my time on the streets had conditioned me to always be ready to protect myself.

Uncle Mike had been a "big bad wolf" for me and had taught me not to trust anybody. Not even Freddy. I heard of too many people winding up in the Indy Downtown City Morgue. I was determined to make sure that I didn't join them. Freddy picked us up in is prized silver Suburban. It was tricked out with 22-inch split spoke chrome wheels. When I finally saw Freddy, he looked so good, I couldn't help but smile. "You look good, Mr. Love", I said as he opened the door for me.

"You do too, Redbone," he replied, "and you smell good enough to eat."

I looked at him and said "Boy, where that come from? You know my brother will kill us both!" He told me how mesmerizing my body was and that he didn't care what Clyde would think. In that instant, I felt like a woman. I had high hopes for a fun night. When we finally got to the club we saw that the line at the door went around the block. Luckily, Freddy knew one of the owners and we were let right in.

All night long, Freddy kept the drinks flowing. Freddy just had to show off and ordered some bottle service for us. He practically had me hypnotized with an endless flow of Hypnotic and Vodka. The DJ rocked some of my favorite tunes that night. I was feeling very good about my prospects with the one and only Mr. Freddy Love. The music was playing and I was high, it felt strange but good at the same time. Freddy was very aggressive with me that night; it was a side of him that I hadn't seen before. He pulled me on the dance floor and waved his hand to the DJ. All of a sudden, "Make It Last Forever" by Keith Sweat came on. While we were dancing he whispered in my ear; "I need you to feel something", he then took my hand and put it on his penis as it bulged out. I felt real horny after touching Freddy's manhood. He had become very appealing to me throughout the course of the night. My girls, meanwhile, were having the time of their lives with Freddy's homeboys.

All night long, the drinks kept coming and blunts never stopped flowing around the table. Freddy wouldn't give me any; his hot breath was constantly blowing sweet and kind words in my ear. My juices had started to flow. Freddy shared while holding me tight that I was his forever. I looked up at him and said "I am fifteen years old. You are twenty-five! I can't be with you!"

I knew something was going wrong. I told Freddy I had to go to the bathroom but he followed me. "You're too sexy" he said, "I'm not letting you out my sight tonight." Next thing I know Freddy was in the bathroom with me locking the door.

When I came out the bathroom stall, Freddy said "I am your bodyguard."

I looked at him and said "yeah, right."

We both laughed but when I turned on the water, my whole world changed. Freddy had sex with me from the back while I was washing my hands. I was in shock but I indulged in this ecstasy. We both seem to enjoy the pleasure of sex in the bathroom. When it was over, Freddy sucked on my ear and said, "I told you you was mine."

I screamed "I am not on birth control!"

He winked at me and said "next time wear some panties, hot girl", then he winked at me again. This had become one hell of a night. Romance in the bathroom equals a baby carriage. We got back to the table everybody was happy. I decided not to drink or smoke no more that night. Nothing went as planned. Freddy was all over me for the rest of the night.

The early mornings really got crazy. Freddy wanted to go in the after-hours joint. We all went with him. He had some drinks put on our table by the waitress. Freddy and his friends went upstairs to gamble. We were there for an hour, then it was raided by the police. Everybody went to jail for something. Ruth picked me up from the Peppermint Juvenile Center late that day. I found out Freddy had to stay in jail for unpaid child support. The judge released me to my parents. If I get in any more trouble girl school would be my only option. I had looked for love in all the wrong places but I was truly in love with Freddy Love.

Ruth knew Freddy through my older brother; they were childhood friends. Freddy promised my brother he would look out for the family while he was in prison. Freddy had always looked out for us money-wise How will the family feel about this grown man being my lover? Freddy was still locked up from the unpaid child support charges. On top of that, the police added drugs, gun, and gambling charges from the club. I wrote him and sent the letters that his cousin had given me. I was trying to understand how this relationship was going to work.

Three months went by. I was sick with stomach cramps but no period. I decided to go to the doctor. "What do you mean I'm pregnant? That is a mistake, Dr. Moore. This is impossible! I have not had sex in three months! My boyfriend's in jail!"

"I'm sorry, Trina," Dr. Moore said, "but the test is accurate that I have performed on you." "I do not want to keep this baby," I replied, "The father is incarcerated. It must be something you can do about this baby! I am not keeping it!"

I soon found myself pregnant with no money and no job. Something had to change. When I wrote Freddy, I told him he was going to be a father again. I needed some help. Freddy was not much on words but he was true to the game. I knew he would do something about our child. Big Ham was Freddy's cousin but they were always together. Freddy was in jail so

Big Ham came to visit me. "Freddy said you have a problem," Big Ham told me, "and you need help getting rid of it."

"I am not getting rid of nothing, Big Ham." I shot back, "It is a life growing in me. I am keeping my baby!"

Big Ham responded "Freddy said you would say that. He sent you five-hundred dollars. He left me with some weed, cocaine, and ecstasy pills. Everything is bagged up and measured. Come to the house tomorrow and be ready to work."

My original territory was off limits to Freddy and his crew. Put Your Hands Up was having trouble excepting that Freddy and I were together. The word on the streets was that my old boyfriend, Chuck, was going to kill Freddy. It will be a cold day in hell before that would happen.

Chapter 3

SOUL TIES - I AM SO ADDICTED TO YOU

I have been fighting depression. When I got with Freddy, my world was good. I did not have to deal with depression, and when he got out of jail he took care of me. When we had our son, he was my hero. Freddy kept me supplied with every alcohol and drug I needed. The sex was fantastic Freddy told me he put an ecstasy pill in my drink when he claimed me as his. I was betrayed once again but pills and alcohol has sustained all my pain. Freddy said I was forever his. One night me and my girls went out. Freddy stayed home to take care of our son. I usually leave the club to go to the After-hours Joint but that night I was so horny from the pills that I decided to go home and have sex with my man. When I pulled up, I saw my best friend's car in my driveway. It was odd because she had called me earlier that night saying she had the cramps and couldn't go out with us. I decided to drive my car to the back and use the back door.

When I opened the door, I heard music playing. I walked slowly through the kitchen. I saw my bedroom door was open. Inside, Lacy was on top of my man giving him the best rodeo ride ever. I was hurt. I thought about killing them both. I went into my son's room, got him and left. I called lacy and said "I hope that ride was worth our friendship! If I ever see you again it will be your last time breathing."

I could not stop crying! I took my son to Ruth's house and decided to make some money to ease the pain. Pigsville always have something going on for the neighborhood. I decided to stop by Big Ham's house to tell him about his cousin that broke my heart. Big Ham had given me a key to his house when Freddy had gone to jail. I never used it then but I thought I would now. He might be sleeping with one of his hood rats that he picks up at the strip club. Well, when I walked through the door and a dice game was going on and Big Ham was talking trash. With the dice in his hand he shouted his "baby needs a pair of shoes". I looked at them all and said "Big Ham, you better not crap out because your little cousin wants a pair too!"

Big Ham laughed and said, "Little Freddy don't want for nothing!"

I winked my eye at him and said "you right, because his damn mother hustles her ass off while his daddy lay on his back."

After my nasty comment, Big Ham decided to shut the crap game down. "Trina, why the hell you at my house using keys in my door without Freddy?" I walked pass everybody didn't say a word went to the kitchen and fixed me a drink. I was no longer high after seeing Freddy and Lacy having the best sex ever. I had turned my cell phone off and told my mother to tell Freddy me and his son staying there. I know once my mother told Freddy I am going to stay with her he thought this would blow over.

I told Big Ham the story of my life and he said "damn girl you can't stay here! My cousin will go crazy that you are staying in a crack house go home and work it out!"

I let Big Ham know it was over "If you don't help me," I told him, "I am going back to Chuck and my original gangster family, PUT YOUR HANDS UP."

Big Ham said "You going to make me and my cousin shut the whole westside of town down, Redbone!"

I knew Big Ham was not playing because he has never called me Redbone. I stayed there for the rest of the early morning and made me some money while Big Ham was sleep. When Big Ham got up he said "did you sleep?"

I looked at him and said "There is money to be made, I don't have time to sleep."

Big Ham said "Your drunk ass knows how to make that money!"

I looked at him and said "You my new supplier. I will not have nothing to do with Freddy!" After that, Big Ham moved me and little Freddy into his condo out North where nobody hangs out at. Freddy was still begging for me to come back home but I told his stupid ass that's Lacy house, not mine.

Six months after my bad break up with Freddy everything was going good. One day, I got a call from my homegirls that Freddy and Big Ham went to jail for drugs. I knew where Big Ham's money was, so I went and bailed both of them out. This was my first time seeing Freddy since I had moved out. I made sure to never be at Ruth's house when Freddy stopped by to pick up little Freddy. I knew Big Ham kept it quiet that he had been taking care of me because Freddy would be upset.

When the trial was over, Freddy had to do five years and Big Ham had to do two years of house arrest for his first offense. I was sad that Freddy had to go to jail but Lacy would be there for him. The word was that he gave her the house while he did his time. Big Ham's condo was in his mother's name so that is where he decided to do his house arrest. I tried to leave the condo but Big Ham said that I needed to stay. I knew in my mind that it was a bad idea. Eventually, I ended up hooking up with Big Ham. We tried to keep it a secret but once I got pregnant we couldn't keep it a secret any longer. This ended his friendship with his cousin, Freddy.

Big Ham and I have two girls together; twins. He loves his girls but he is such a lady's man. I sit at home and makes all the money. One thing for sure, when Freddy sent me money and drugs by Big Ham, I knew I would never be broke again. That was five years ago. I feel like what goes around will come around. Freddy did four years and when he came home, he tried to make my life a living hell. But Big Ham wasn't having it. Even though I had been so in love with Freddy at one point, our interactions had become completely toxic.

One day, while at the house talking with Big Ham, my phone started ringing. I knew it was Freddy calling. I answered his call and we immediately started arguing. I could hear him scream "Bitch, I want to see my son!" Then, Freddy started calling me names. I knew we were going nowhere. It has been six years since we been together. He couldn't get over the fact that I had moved on with my life. Freddy angrily hung up but called right back. This time however, Big Ham grabbed the phone and answered it. But it only added more fuel to the fire. "Hello bro. what's up?" Big Ham said,"I could hear from the phone. Fuck you, man."

Freddy quickly fired back; "You can have that bitch and the two kids you had together. I'm coming for my son!" then he hung up. I don't know why Freddy's so mad that Big Ham and I had gotten together. I don't care they are cousins; If his daddy had money I would have fucked him too.

Somebody had to take care of me and my son. Big Ham think's he is slick but I am slick with him. Chuck and I are still close: he is my side kick. I can't let him go because he was my first love. Without him Uncle Mike would still be having sex with me. Chuck had my back when nobody else would. He had the downtown area locked down. Chuck had a girlfriend and she was cool. Our relationship was strictly a friendship. I always made sure Chuck was safe and he did the same for me. Sex was no longer a factor with me and Chuck. Sometimes we would get a hotel room and wild out.

Chapter 4

Depression - Disloyalty with in me

After a while, Big Ham and I began to truly have some problems. We both were drinking and popping pills. Fighting had become a regular routine for us. I started leaving the children over at Ruth's house. Big Ham and I had a love/hate relationship. It started when I told him that I only got with him to hurt Freddy. Big Ham started getting high and flipping out on me. Drugs and alcohol stop working for my depression. I thought about killing myself. I didn't want to live anymore. I went to the crack house and worked for three days straight just to keep busy and not get my ass beat. I took my weekend money I made and rented me a house for me and the children.

Pigsville was my hood. I did not want to move out the hood. I needed to be close to Ruth. I had professional movers move my belongings out of Big Ham's condo. I had to be out before he came home that night from the strip club. The movers set my house up nice so I tipped them one hundred dollars. I really need to change my life. One of Ruth's friends always took us to church when we were little. Ruth would work seven days a week. I started having second thoughts about killing myself. Moving into my new place definitely helped me to see a more positive side of my life. Thank You God. I was doing well on my own.

Another year went by. I had been living the good life just with my children. My kids spent lots of time at Ruth's house. One day, I decided to pick them up and go grocery shopping. We got to the store and had just walked in when I saw Lacy. I kept my head high and kept walking with the children in my cart. As we passed her, Lacy, the home wrecker, spoke to little Freddy. When she did that, something came over me and I snapped! I went up to her and grabbed her weave and started to beat her in the face. Lacy tried to hit back but I would pull her hair even harder. The children were crying saying "mommy, stop!" I was hurt so bad, I needed to take it out on somebody, so why not Lacy? Security and employees started breaking up the fight then I remembered blacking out. When I regained consciousness, the police begin to read me my rights. They had found drugs, money and a gun on me. Child Protection Service took my children. They were crying while the police put me in handcuffs. In just a few moments, my life had turned upside down; Lacy was going to the hospital and I was going to prison.

Two days later in the Peppermint County Jail, I was speaking with my lawyer. "How dare this whore speak to my child!" I shouted.

The lawyer responded "Are you listening to me, Ms. Right? Battery is considered a Class B Misdemeanor. This criminal offense carries 180 days. You had a gun permit so that will not be held against you. You had more than 30 grams of marijuana in your purse; it is a Class D felony it can carry up to 3 years along with the pills found. Ms. Trina your children are in foster care. You going to do some jail time."

I looked at him and said "What the hell you are getting paid for if I can't beat this case?"

This criminal attorney, Mr. Black, was known to be one of the best in the state of Indiana. He needed to find a way to keep me out of jail. He can give my two-thousand dollars back if I am going to sit in hell.

When the attorney left and I realized that my children had a better chance in the welfare system then with their foolish fathers. I had stopped talking to Big Ham before this jail situation because one of our daughters said to me "daddy licked my vagina." I told her "daddy would not do that. Please don't say that again." My twins Sha and Sasha were very smart children, even at just at five years old. I knew that nasty hound, Big Ham, had touched his daughter. But I was too ashamed to tell anybody. I kept them away from Big Ham. It felt like I was cursed. I felt like giving up.

Eventually, the psychiatrist came to see me. I had been telling people that I wanted to kill myself. He only asked me a few questions. "Have you ever tried to hurt yourself?"

"Yes," I replied, "I am really depressed and in jail. I want my kids back.

I had tried to kill myself a couple of times at home with pills and slashing my wrist."

The psychiatrist responded in a low voice: "Do you want to hurt others?"

"Yes, I do!" I snapped back.

"Who would you like to hurt?"

"All men that hurt me."

"You are suffering from heavy depression." he said "I will be putting in an order to get you help."

I told him "Thank you. Take your ass home to your family. Tell the judge that." I laughed in his face. "Get out my cell."

In jail there were church services twice a week. I started going to them. I really didn't think anything would transpire from serving the Lord but my life had really changed. I had found the true and living God. I decided to get baptized in jail. The nurse brought my medication to me every day. I prayed that my mental illness would leave me. I started studying the word of God in bible study. I was really hurt about my children having a new family. But I was behind bars and couldn't do much. Meanwhile, Ruth was dealing with Clyde's prison drama and more family secrets came out; Mark had been unfaithful to Ruth. Mark had had a child named Kenya with Ms. Wanda years ago. Kenya came to live with my mom six years ago.

Kenya was as good as my sister. She is twenty years old now. Kenya had a little girl of her own, Chloe, who was four years old and always played with my children. Chloe was younger than the twins. I wanted Ruth to take my children but it was too chaotic at her house. Ruth had left Mark years ago but Kenya stayed. Ruth put up with so much shit from Mark with all of his other women. Ruth also had to deal with my older brother; his prison life was hard on her. Clyde stayed in prison. Ruth was so strong; she had taken me on as her own child. Nobody knew about Mark's illegitimate child with Wanda until one day, she left him with the baby; she said she was going to the grocery store to get some cornmeal to fry the fish he had caught earlier that morning. Ms. Wanda never came back. Now Mark knows what a bitch life can be! Mark had to bring the bastard child home to Ruth. The same game Mark played with Ruth about going fishing, Ms. Wanda played with him.

Mark's daughter Kenya Right just graduated from cosmetology school.

Kenya became a teenage mother but Ruth helped her. Now it is paying off. Kenya called Ruth mom. She knew that made me mad. I told her "Your mom's name is Wanda and we still waiting on her black ass to come back to pick you up."

Ruth would tell me "That is your sister! Stop saying hellish things to her."

I would come back and say "Mom, every year you reveal a secret; this better not be my sister! This is one crazy family!" The ghetto is real. Pigsville Gang for life!

The judge had given me two years in jail but my lawyer had talked with the judge for me to do a drug program and community service. I did six months in jail as time served. I was so happy my children could visit me in rehab. My children were well taken care of. I was happy that my children loved their foster parents but they had to know it was just temporary placement. I was their damn mother! My priority was getting back my children!

Chapter 5

HAUGHTY - THE PRIDE IN US WANT DIE.

After I found God my life started looking up. I got my GED in jail. Once I got out of jail, I started working at a nursing home as a CNA. I finally got my children back. It was not easy but the hard work paid off. Love is so crazy. Freddy and I got back together. He works and helps with all three children. It had been two years since Freddy and I gave our love a second try. It was rocky. Freddy eventually decided to join my church. His church was Baptist and my belief had changed in jail. The bible was too powerful for me to be tied down to one religion. Freddy said church is church. I loved my church. Jake and Lynda Gray were my pastors. They brought life to me at Free in God Church. One day, Pastor Jake and his wife called a meeting with us. They told us that we could not stay in their church while living in sin. Pastor Jake stated "You need to marry or leave each other alone." Freddy told Pastor Jake that he wanted to marry me. Pastor Jake said, "Well, young man, let's get this celebration started!"

My sister's daughter, Chloe, stayed over all the time because she loved going to church with us. It would have been a misfortune for Chloe if we would have been expelled from the church. I didn't want her to lose faith in God. When I was in jail, Freddy began to get himself together. He had kept a job for two years. The miracle was that Freddy had given his life to God. Freddy and I started talking again while I was in jail. We both wanted to work things out for the children. I was so joyful that Freddy wanted me as his wife.

Freddy took me to a Keith Sweat concert. We had first row seats. During a break in his set, Keith Sweat announced to the crowd; "Ms. Trina can you please join me on stage? I have a special request for you."

I looked around and said "I know this is not real."

Freddy said, "Go on stage, girl. Don't keep Keith Sweat waiting."

I looked around and saw that nobody was moving. As I was walking towards the stage, the music started playing. It was "Make it Last Forever"; the song Freddy and I had first made love to. Freddy came on stage and took the microphone while Keith was singing but Keith kept singing harder. "Redbone", Freddy began, "without you there is no me. You make my world complete."

When Freddy came with a diamond ring in a shape of a heart, I thought I would need sunglasses on stage; it was blinging. My body got so hot for him. I screamed "Yes! I'll marry you!" We kissed, everybody in the audience were screaming, whistling, and saying "yes".

The audience was clapping as Keith took the microphone back. He sang the hell out of our song. We got off stage and enjoyed the rest of our night with Keith Sweat. I felt so in love that night. I told Freddy to take me home so I can practice being Mrs. Love. I knew it was time to settle down; this man was sending chills down my body. Freddy got sexed up all night. We had some incredible sex after the concert but I had told Freddy we were not going to have sex again until after the wedding. Between the ring and being serenaded at a Keith Sweat concert, Freddy could have begged anyone out of their clothes. I had to repent and move on.

Freddy and I both had some secrets we were keeping from each other. Both of us needed spiritual guidance before we could truly say "I do". The brothers at the church became Freddy's new friends. His gang life was finally at an end. The brothers of the church would take Freddy out on weekends to keep him on the right path. We would have youth night twice a month on a Friday where the youth would gather and play games, basketball and dance contests this kept us involved with our children. We were enjoying life and preparing for our big wedding day. The time was flying by so fast, so we decided that my bachelorette party should be held the Friday before the wedding.

We decided to have one big weekend wedding party at the Hills Hotel. I warned everybody invited I was still a work in progress; "do not come if you going to judge me," I thought. I did not, however, invite my pastor's wife; she would not understand the whore in my lifestyle. I knew a few of the church women still liked to party and so I invited the whole praise team. They knew how to balance having a good time with praising the Lord. The girls knew God and could lead the whole congregation into worship, but on their spare time they knew the way to the liquor store. I really hoped that the chattering women of the church didn't come to my party because I was prepared to give them something to talk about! My circle at the church was small but the praise team shared almost everything with each other.

My two homegirls, Cree and Savanna, were in charge of planning the party. They were good friends and I knew that they would keep me laughing. I did, however, have to warn them that my church family will be there and that they needed to respect them. I really didn't drink anymore but I still needed to have my daily cigarettes and coffee. I told Cree and Savanna that the only drinks I wanted at the reception was wine, margaritas, daiquiris, and Mexican beer. I planned on drinking on my wedding night but I might have a few drinks on my last night being single. Freddy and I had planned on a small, intimate wedding. Now we both wanted to party apart on our last night being single.

Freddy suggested that we should both be at the same hotel since we will be getting married there. I agreed and told him "Nobody will be late for our special day. I don't care if their ass is drunk and hungover; there is no excuse." My girls and I got together to plan my bachelorette party together. The theme "Pimp and Hoes" made me so excited. The ladies were to dress up as beautiful call girls and the "pimps" were coming straight from Atlanta Georgia; the finest from Diamond Big and Black Male Review Strip Club.

Three weeks had passed by and Freddy and I had not had sex in anticipation for the wedding. The tension was so bad I decided to stay over at Kenya's house. My sister and I always bumped heads when we could not agree. The week of the wedding had come so quick. I set up a spa date with my bridal party for Friday. I thought about Lacy. I really had missed her since my life had changed in jail. I wanted her to be a part of this happy time of my life. The friendship ended over Freddy. My inconsiderate ass went to jail for attacking her. I was glad jail had changed my life by leading me to God. I wanted to invite her to my party but I was never to have contact with Lacy again. My girlfriends were going be with me for my special day. Friends were everything for me, especially on my wedding day. Octavia, Harmony, and Angel were new friends from the church that had agreed to help set up for the bachelorette party.

We ordered a penthouse suite with additional rooms for my bridesmaids. My sister Kenya paid for this bachelorette party. It cost her over two thousand dollars. My sister has never been cheap when it came to doing things for me and the children. I had always loved Kenya as a sister and I had loved her daughter, Chloe, as my own child. I felt bad because, growing up, I never did anything for Kenya but tease her about her real mother, Ms. Wanda. I remember taunting her, saying "She still at the grocery store getting corn meal and cooking grease! When will your mother be picking your grown ass up?"

Although I had teased her for years, I knew that Kenya always had my back. It certainly helped that Kenya's baby daddy was a big-time marijuana dealer in Pigsville. My sister wanted for nothing in life. The hotel gave us a discount on everything because we are staying four days and three nights with six rooms plus the penthouse. The wedding was outside in the courtyard; it was so beautiful that time of the year. September is just right for being in love and having a wedding outside. The sun shined all over the yard and the wind that blew the trees brought such fresh air in the courtyard.

Everybody I knew pitched in to help out for the wedding, even Big Ham. His black ass wasn't even invited to the wedding. I can't believe I gave his ass twin girls. He was such a hoe and a dead beat. I knew his nasty ass gave me herpes while I was with him. I just left that alone but if he touches me or my daughters again, I will kill his motherfucking ass. Nevertheless, I was glad to hear that he gave Freddy five thousand dollars. He said for the girls wedding attire. Who knows what the hell he thought the girls would wear for a wedding that cost five thousand dollars. The original cost of the wedding was twenty-five thousand dollars for the total weekend.

Cree worked at the hotel as one of the front desk clerk agents and was able to get us an excellent price. Cree's aunt was the manager of the hotel, so we were very lucky. Cree used her employee discount that gave us the deal of a lifetime. The hotel served food and drinks for the spa party, bachelorette party, and wedding reception. We paid a total of $15,000 for the entire weekend. God loved me enough to bring me and Freddy together. We were glad to share our joy with friends and family. We had both been through hell but heaven had finally come into our lives and saved us. And to make things even better, the hotel had given us complimentary spa and message treatments. After weeks of planning, preparing, and building sexual tension, my wedding weekend finally arrived.

I was so excited to be getting married to my first love that weekend but I was ready to party as a free woman for one last time that Friday night. Come Sunday morning, I would be known as Mrs. Trina Love.

I anticipated that Freddy and his boys would have fun because the girls and I were going to take the roof off this hotel. We would show the people how to party. I did not have anything to worry about. My church girls were with me; the best praise team in Pigsville. Sadly, only three of the girls would be attending. I heard the chatter ladies at the church were saying that whoever attended my party would die and go to hell. I told them to share with my church family that God had our backs. Nothing is wrong with a little fun before committing to a lifetime of marriage. The day of the party finally came. I greeted all my guests with "Thank God It Is Friday", and in response, I got a resounding "Party time!" from my loyal group of friends.

The bride and groom party spa adventure had begun! I hoped that we could all get along to enjoy this time together. I asked myself "Can the church crowd and the gangbangers all get along for our special day?" Luckily, everything went exactly as planned we all checked into the hotel after 6:00 pm. I did a count to make sure all our friends, family, and special guests had arrived and checked in. When Freddy and I were done counting, we realized that we had thirty people that we would be responsible for the whole weekend. We looked at each other and said "How did we get up to thirty people?" We both laughed and said "Let's get this party started!" The pastor and his wife were gracious enough to make a generous contribution to us for the wedding. Pastor Lynda had already agreed to be a part of the spa preparation. She had given me a five hundred dollars visa gift card.

This wedding planning had been so overwhelming for me. I hoped this whore in me would die. I didn't want to let my new church family down. They had been really good to me and my family. They were my support system. We had wine and beer for our Friday night luxury spa encounter. Everybody was delighted with their facials, waxing, manicure, pedicures, and body massages. It was pure pleasure. I was so ready for the bachelorette party to begin. I was feeling so beautiful. I raised my voice and shared it with everyone within earshot. Everyone answered back in agreement. There was so much love in the air. Everybody was sipping on their drinks. I had a little glass of wine. I knew not to let myself get out of control in front of the pastor and his wife.

Chapter 6

Blindness - Addicted to You

Before our parties started, Freddy called my room. He said, "Can I see you before the party, my sexy Redbone? I just want one kiss and to feel what I will be getting tomorrow night from my bride."

I started giggling and grinning like when we first meet. Chills came over my body. I was ready to skip the party and become one with him. I said "Mr. Love why are you getting me hot for you? You playing with my emotions! Do you really want two thousand dollars to be wasted?"

Freddy said, "Trina don't push me; all this is for you, not me. I wanted to go to the justice of the peace. You've been holding sex from me a whole month. I just want to touch you. Why you acting like we our brand-new to this love affair? I'm yours Mr. Freddy Love. You keep chills going through my body since our first date.

"Freddy," I replied, "now we going to do it the right way. No cheating; just me and you and the children."

Freddy said "I'm going to let you off the hook for now. You will be my wife tomorrow and we going to make a baby. I am going to love on you all night long until daylight hit."

"Freddy," I fired back "after I put this married sex on you, you will be out like a light in thirty minutes." We both started laughing so hard.

Freddy said "I give up, Redbone. I am getting ready to get dressed to hang with the boys."

When I arrived to my bachelorette party everything was so alluring. This will be a great night to end as Ms. Trina Right. I felt so sexy in my see-through dress. I got in my feelings and did my famous cat walk to the bar. The music was jumping and all my friends were there dancing around, enjoying themselves. I looked around and I saw gifts everywhere. A waiter walked up to me and said "Ms. Trina Right, you are a very attractive woman!"

I said "thank you."

He said "I am to escort you to your seat."

My best friends were standing around the table to greet me. I had me a screwdriver cocktail in my hand. Nothing too powerful but enough to get this party started. My girls had a chair decorated with Bride-To-Be across the seat waiting for me. I was crowned with a tiara to match. We had a wonderful time from the beginning to end.

Bella started the games. The first one was "Pin the condom on the penis". Freddy's mother Capri was the winner of that game. Kenya had made jello shots and a game to go along with them. We were getting intoxicated. Next thing we did was eat. I had never seen so much food in my life. The hotel really took care of us. I am glad we had a cash bar, though. Everybody had plenty of money to drink. My sister called out my name: "Trina! It is time for your gifts." I could not believe all the money people spent on me. I received over a thousand dollars' worth of gift cards.

My favorite gifts were night clothes. I got about ten gowns and some erotic robes. My sister brought me twenty bra and panty sets from Victoria Secrets. We were laughing at some of the panties. My sister said, I wanted it to be little of the imagination. We were having so much fun. Then it was time for the cake! This big dark chocolate penis came out with half naked men carrying the cake. The men set the cake down and we all just enjoyed the view. Everybody was having a good time. Next the regular lights went off and the sparkles from the party lights gleamed all over the room. My favorite song from my past came on. "Wild Wild West".

On to the stage, these four exotic men came out dressed as cowboys. Very sexy men. My girls and I started laughing and getting into the fast groove of the music. I loved old-school rap. It was so much cleaner than the modern rap. The men got on the mic and stated their names. Lenard, "Leo the Lion", Blade, known as "Chocolate Thunder", Daran, known as "Mr. President", Calvin, known as "Black Diamond", and we had DJ Kirk playing the music all night long. We all had so much fun throughout the night. The gentleman announced this would be their last performance for the night. "We flew all the way from Atlanta City known as the Chocolate City just for you Trina Right. Turn up!"

`We have a special treat for Ms. Trina "Introducing Chocolate Thunder"!

The music started playing as this dark, fine-looking man started walking towards my chair. He was tall and thick built with braids going down his back. He looked good enough for me to eat.

The song by Ginuwine "My Pony" started playing all I could hear were the lyrics of the beginning of the song:

"If you're horny, let's do it
Ride it, my pony
My saddle's waiting
Come and jump on it..."

This sexy chocolate pulled me up out my seat. He was lip singing and grinding his body on mine. His penis was huge. I became wet between the legs. Everybody was cheering and rooting him on. The strange part was I loved every minute of it. He whispered in my ear "Would you like to ride on my pony?" His hot breath had my juices running. Next thing I know, he went up my dress and touched my juicy. He said, "Yes, Trina you ready to ride."

By the end of the song Chocolate Thunder had worked me all up in and out of my chair. This man has taken me to paradise. That was the end of the show. I gave it five stars. Chocolate Thunder came up to me and shared he would love the pleasure of walking me to my room. I told him follow me. There was little talk on the way there.

We got to my door. I asked him, would he like to come in for a drink. We both knew he was coming in for the night. Yes! Would you like a private show for tonight! You don't have to ask, I thought. Let the rodeo begin. "Blame it on the Alcohol" is all I could say. Chocolate Thunder stuck his tongue in my mouth. He swirled his tongue with mine. We exchanged salvia with each other while his hands removed my dress. We both where standing there naked, caressing each other's bodies. Before I knew it, we were exchanging sexual favors in the heat of the moment. I rode that pony half the night.

I gave Chocolate Thunder a tip and sent him on his way. Got back in my bed and tried to replay what the hell did I just do. The sex was off the map. I did not know that man. Our souls connected like we had been lovers forever. I must stop putting myself in situations that allow me to lose control. This onetime affair will make me look Chocolate Thunder up on my next vacation to the Chocolate City.

Chapter 7

Marriage - King of Baal

Today is the day I will become Mrs. Freddy Love my heart skips a thousand beats. My love is like a ship in the ocean. Last night was my last night single and the best time I ever had. This bachelorette party will always be on my top 5 parties because my new friend the lead stripper Blade A.K.A Chocolate Thunder had my ship sinking in the ocean. I could only say, Captain Thunder the storm is too much can you have your boys throw in the anchor. Wow me and my bridal party and church girls had a time of our life. If it wasn't for my pastor and wife telling me and Freddy we had to get married or leave the church. I would be riding my pony Black Thunder all the way back to Atlanta and leave Freddy and the kids.

I must stop this crazy thinking! I am getting married in six hours. All my life I have felt unloved but tonight I am going to be like, "Keith Sweat Make It Last forever".

I will be Mrs. Freddy Love. My theme had changed over the past few weeks for the wedding. I have had so many mixed emotions about the wedding. I changed the color three times the theme has been up in the air for debate by my wedding crew. When it came to me and Freddy I decided he had found me in my darkest place. I found him in his darkest place. Diamond in the Rough became the theme for my wedding day. I really wanted everything be sort of dark. I would be the light bright that would shine through the night. The color choices were black, silver, sequences, studs and diamonds. My bridesmaids helped pull the weekend off.

When Freddy gave me that diamond ring shaped in a heart I knew I had been found. It is time to shine as Freddy love queen. Here is the moment. Wow! I am the one. It is time for my dad to walk me down to Freddy. My dress was so beautiful it was a white strapless fitted chiffon dress with rhinestones and sequin with a split on the side with my back out. I wore 3in heels that were made with rhinestones that the sparkles enhanced my dress with diamond accents. The courtyard was so beautiful my bridesmaids had on elegant charcoal chiffon strapless dress with 4in silver heels sling backs. The men had on all black suits with charcoal grey shoes and ties. My dad was so happy that me and Freddy was getting married everybody liked him. My problems I had in the past with Freddy is forgotten. The music has started. If my family could have got me married to this man years ago they would have. Freddy and my oldest brother were best friends but he was not happy. I still don't understand how my parents approved of me with this grown man as a child. I am all grown up now with children.

My dad said to me, my daughter it is time to say goodbye as my little girl are you ready? Yes! Next my dad had me moving so fast down the walkway. I am thinking about the past and last night this shit got me scared! This crazy man known as my father should feel his precious daughter shaking her ass off. I feel like my dad is saying please take this trouble child off my hands so I can go find Ms. Wanda ass at the grocery store! I started laughing so hard my dad looked at me and I had to pull myself together and get back to my own wedding. The song "You by Jesse Powell "was playing almost missed half my wedding song laughing at nothing but a thought. When I got next to my man the lyrics that were floating in the air, I'm giving all my love away and there's only one reason that I would. And baby it's you. Tears were coming down my face and my husband in the making reached out and held my hand and winked his left eye to assure me that everything was good. The song finished. Our vowels started. My pastor asked was there anybody against this couple becoming husband and wife?

I said please don't let one of Freddy crazy baby mamas say yes. It was so quiet! The pastor said, now I pronounce you Mr. And Mrs. Freddy Love! You may kiss your bride. The audience were clapping and blowing bubbles while my husband gave me the kiss of a lifetime. I love this man Lord! Last night let me know that Freddy better step up his love game in the bedroom because Chocolate Thunder is just a phone call away.

We did not have a honeymoon we just enjoyed family and friends all weekend at the hotel. We party hard at the reception the music was rocking DJ King and DJ Queen were tag teaming the music. I looked up and seen my girls had kept our little stripper friends around. The shocking part was Chocolate Thunder kept looking at me. I would look over at the table and he was blowing kisses at me. I am always getting myself in trouble but this man better not ruin my first night as Mrs. Freddy Love. My husband was whispering sweet nothings in my ear while Chocolate Thunder was sitting across the room winking his eyes at me. We need to talk before this reception turn into a war zone. I knew to say a quick prayer.

Dear God, it is me your daughter Trina who can't stop getting in trouble! If you get me out of this drama tonight I will be faithful to Freddy until death do us part Aman. Cree and Savanna came over to our table and shared they was on their way to the airport to drop their dates off and they would be back in a couple of hours. Wow God that was fast!

Thank you God I did not know you would move that quick! Freddy did not know we had strippers at the bachelorette party. I just didn't tell him because he would want to be there watching my every move. Freddy has a healthy sexual appetite his fantasy is to be with me and another woman. If my secret got out it just might happen for him. We wanted to end the night of our marriage becoming one as Mr. And Mrs. Freddy Love with a tattoo party in the penthouse. Over the years we had put tattoos on our bodies but never to connect our love. Being in church has changed my thinking and the bible tells us not to mark our bodies. I was going to get my six tattoos removed but Freddy was against it. Now that we are married he want me to demonstrate my love with a new tattoo showing our unity. My husband the "Great Freddy Love" controls my every move! I think that is why I married this man today.

We had plenty of people stay after the reception that wanted tattoos. I was shocked when Sister Harmony wanted an Infinity symbol with love and music in the infinity. I told Harmony you know you lead the choir and pastor is not going to be happy. Her respond was. I am putting it on my lower back what pastor don't know want hurt him or the choir. Freddy and Harmony laughed! I looked at her and said you out of order and shook my head. The tattoo party was a success we brought music to the penthouse from the reception thanks to our own DJ King and DJ Queen from Naptown City. This couple has been working together and producing beats for years. I was so elated that paying the extra five hundred dollars to get the couple to stay for the tattoo party was a privilege. It was like having superstars sharing our special wedding day.

We had four tattoo artists at the party and eight people stayed to get tattoos plus me and Freddy. I told my husband if I want to get something meaningfully. If I do go to hell it was for my husband. This fool tried to talk me into getting chess pieces. I said, do our marriage look like a damn game to you Freddy Love? I don't play chess! We almost got a divorced four hours into the marriage. I said Freddy why in the hell would we get King and Queen pieces what is romantic about that? I don't know shit about chess everybody was looking at us and Savannah said chill out newlyweds. Me and my husband apologized to our guest and decided to get an open puzzle piece with red ink and black writing with Mr. And Mrs. Freddy Love. After everybody left I said a prayer: Lord forgive me why is this man so controlling and I do what he tells me to do. I am sorry I keep hurting my body. Aman! I went to bed and told my new husband sex was out! My arm hurts. How dare him curse me out in front of our wedding guest this was a big mistake. I promised God I would stay with him even if it kills me or him.

Chapter 8

Deliverance - What's love got to do with it

That night of my black eye I knew it was time to really make a change in my life. I had a meeting with my pastor the next day. I was used as a punching bag. I could not waste no time. I said, I was going to leave this man he was always angry at his family. I had to wear sun glasses to cover my pain. Pastor ask me how I was feeling? I took off my sunglasses and said not to good. I can only see out one eye. Pastor eyes got big and he immediately started praying in tongues and pleading the blood. I got scared because pastor never acted holy before in or out of church. His wife always did the fighting in the spirit she was truly a godly woman.

Daughter! he yelled with a loud voice is the family hurt? I said, no! Pastor just me this time. What do you mean this time? Well he has put his hands on me and the children multiple times. I hope you not sharing with me there is domestic abuse in the house. We will not let this continue. Pastor I am going to tell the truth when Freddy not there we all can breathe. When he is home I am walking on eggshells. The children are all out of control. I am praying for him to take his butt to bed early every night. He does work hard. Pastor said, I work hard to Sister Trina there is no excuse for his actions! We do not put our hand on women or children at this church.

I had to let pastor know my husband is good most of the time. He does all the housework, yard work, and cooking. I love Freddy for that but these periodically mood swings must stop. I agree with you pastor. I am ready to leave him. I can do bad all by myself. My pastor suggested to go through healing and deliverance sessions without Freddy. I ask is that an exorcism? Pastor said yes, you will be releasing a lot of your hurt and pain through Christ Jesus. Pastor started giving me orders. I was listen closely because I was scared. I never heard of this but through television and watching scary movies. Pastor was talking so fast I could not say yes sir fast enough. Sister Trina I need you to connect with Sister Yvette at the church she will be the minister that will be praying for you daily. My children and I moved out of the house and Mother Ruth home I went.

Freddy need to be healed. I know he has childhood hurt that has lead his life of constant violence. I thought Freddy was being healed in church from rejection. He had been faithful in participating with the men weekend outings. Hopefully things will daily change for me with my accountability partner Minister Yvette. Pastor Lynda and the mothers of the church will be working closely with me. Until I am ready to release all the hurt and pain. I'm carrying such a burden in my heart since I was a little girl.

Pastor called another meeting this time with his wife present. Pastor Jake was not happy. Pastor said, I tell you this much Sister Trina if Brother Freddy don't get it together. I will be putting him out of this church. His violence must be put under control. Physically abusing people, it is not allowed. It is unacceptable in the house of God. When I left my meeting. I went home and cleaned up. I went in the kitchen and it was flowers with a card. My mother said, your wonderful husband stopped by. Freddy has me so mad. I love him at the same time. Why do I get flowers from him giving me a black eye? I am going to pretend we all good. I know somebody going to perish just like the flowers he brought. If my husband thinks my face is his punching bag.

I started hanging out at church with Sister Yvette. I would call Sister Yvette when I would struggle with being a Christian. Sister Yvette would tell me some of her stories about being in captivity with the devil. She had really become my prayer partner. My children and I would be at church while Freddy would be at home complaining. After six months of consistency trusting God for change. I went back home to Freddy. My marriage to Freddy started to change. He started coming to church just as much as the children and I. My family life became pretty good. I decided to go through forgiveness deliverance. I was told this would start my life over again. I ask Freddy to do one. He said no, I love everybody. We looked at each other and laughed.

Pastor Lynda had put a team together to take me through deliverance. Prayer and fasting were going on all week. My family were also told to fast and have prayer together. My problems all came from rejection of both biological parents giving me away. My identity became interrupted when Uncle Mike violated me. Pastor Lynda told me my roots were deep from my mother's womb. In the natural life the doctor would say, I had a personality disorder. Pastor Lynda said, we are going to start with scriptures that will start your forgiveness. I have written the scriptures down for you. They will be very important to you in your life Trina. Carry these scriptures with you.

Pastor Lynda and the ladies of the church started the prayer meeting and that day March 06, 2008 I became set free. I was a new creature in Christ Jesus. Trina can you read your scriptures out loud so the devil will know you are healed. If he brings anymore chaos to your life again you have the word of God to fight your battle.

Trina Love Deliverance Scriptures

1. For if you forgive other people when they sin against you, your heavenly Father will also forgive you. But if you do not forgive others their sins, your Father will not forgive your sins. Matthew 6:14-15 NIV
2. Love is patient, love is kind. It does not envy, it does not boast, it is not proud. It does not dishonor others, it is not self-seeking, it is not easily angered, it keeps no record of wrongs. It always protects, always trusts, always hopes, always perseveres. 1 Corinthians 13:4-5, 7 NIV
3. Submit yourselves, then, to God. Resist the devil, and he will flee from you. James 4:7NIV
4. You, my brothers and sisters, were called to be free. But do not use your freedom to indulge the flesh; rather, serve one another humbly in love. If you bite and devour each other, watch out or you will be destroyed by each other. So I say, walk by the Spirit, and

> you will not gratify the desires of the flesh. For the flesh desires what is contrary to the Spirit, and the Spirit what is contrary to the flesh. They are in conflict with each other, so that you are not to do whatever you want. But if you are led by the Spirit, you are not under the law. The acts of the flesh are obvious: sexual immorality, impurity and debauchery; idolatry and witchcraft; hatred, discord, jealousy, fits of rage, selfish ambition, dissensions, factions and envy; drunkenness, orgies, and the like. I warn you, as I did before, that those who live like this will not inherit the kingdom of God. But the fruit of the Spirit is love, joy, peace, forbearance, kindness, goodness, faithfulness, Those who belong to Christ Jesus have crucified the flesh with its passions and desires. Since we live by the Spirit, let us keep in step with the Spirit. Let us not become conceited, provoking and envying each other. Galatians 5:13, 15-22, 24-26 NIV

The tree of my life was big and had overpowered me. I kept coming to church until I became a new me. I was told to never go back to drinking, drugs, smoking and using heavy profanity again. Surround myself with people that loved God like me. The last thing I was taught was to use my bible for all my problems. Never open any doors up again because the devil will walk through to steal, kill, and destroy me. The doors of sin will stay closed with God word. You will stay victorious Trina! Pastor Lynda said. Pay your tithes and give to others. This is very important you can't beat God giving no matter how you try. If you fall short and become weak please call your prayer partner Sister Yvette. Please call me and pastor if you need us.

Chapter 9

Church Hurt - Who living right in the church house

My husband decided to start his own church. It had been seven years of a life changed experience from God. I knew my husband had changed his life he had not been to jail in over fifteen years. We had both started living a Godly life. Gang banging was the past for me and him. I hope Freddy had put drugs and alcohol behind him to. I think he get high but if he is playing with God he will be struck down. Looking back at me and Freddy life you would not think we would be serving God. It was not common for past gangbangers to spread the good news. I preached to my congregation about my deliverance. I did not desire to be a whore anymore. I stopped smoking drugs, popping pills, drinking alcohol and my love for God became stronge. I tried to hold on to the good faith of salvation but so many adversities would come my way. I had worked hard to get to this point in my life but being the First Lady of a church that was named after me had put me up on a pedestal that I don't like.

Aunt Raelin and Mother Capri handled collecting the money at the church. Freddy had them answering the phones for emergency situations and the prayer line. Freddy was working on starting his childcare ministry at the church. He told me to go part time as a nurse and run the daycare. I said, no! I love my own bread and butter let your mother and aunt handle that ministry. Freddy listen to me for the first time and his family started a family daycare ministry. My children were doing their own thing getting in trouble and causing hell in the house. The oldest son got high all the time. Freddy act like he didn't care. Freddy wanted to put all the children out. I said no! The twins decided to go live with their father Big Ham. I could not stop the girls they had become rebellious teenagers. They thought they knew everything.

My niece had stop staying with us two months ago because her and my husband was not getting along and Kenya told her to come and live with her. I hate that my niece had to live with drug pushers. We were once drug dealers and Kenya knew what happened to us. My past still haunting me and my children. Greed and hurt put my children in foster care. I pray that it doesn't happen to Kenya. My sister called me about a couple of fights that broke out at the house between Freddy and the girls. One incident the twins jumped in to help Chole and all three girls beat Freddy up. I believe they are hiding the true purpose of the fight. He went to bible study that night like nothing happened. He preached like a mad man. Over twenty-five young people got saved that night.

I told Kenya, I hope everybody heals from this family drama. I was at work I don't know too much about the disturbances. I am glad Chloe safe with you. Freddy told me all three of the girls jumped him because he gave orders to clean the kitchen and bathroom. Kenya, please call my husband. Not me! I hung up the phone my sister did not call back and it was not brought up again.

Summer Sunday Healing services had started in our lot with a big tent. We had fun during this time of the year. We have been serving the community for five years. During the festivities Pigsville best bakery on the west side donates us with juice, coffee, and donuts. Church would be large over two hundred people each Sunday. Having this summer revival that represents our five-year anniversary of the church. Pastor Freddy had four people that took care of the church, Deacon Miles, Deacon Nash, and Assistant Pastor Kent Bush and his wife Robin. The Bush family were beautiful people. Pastor Jake sent them to assist with the church five years ago. Church is still running professionally. We are so thankful to their loyalty and the covering of our church Pastor Jake.

The church was doing well we had one hundred members that joined the church. It was getting close to our ending summer festival, church outside in a tent! The members in the choir had been practicing for our last big celebration that was coming up. Rehearsals and meetings were happening daily. Hospitality group was led by Bella Freddy sister. Some rumors had started about my husband. Bella told me what they were saying. She is the leader of the hospitality group and that was her brother. Bella came to me so sweet but honest. I hate to tell on my brother. Trina, I love you as a sister. Freddy was seen out to dinner with a very young lady from the church that had a baby he was holding. I will handle this Bella! I will have a talk with my husband.

The leader of the church should not be out with a woman and child without his wife. As the first lady, I had to go to my husband and tell him about his self. I went home took a shower and got in bed. Freddy was helping our youngest son with his homework. I decided to talk to him in the morning. I am too tired to argue. Next day I got up an hour early and cooked breakfast for my husband. Pastor Freddy Love came downstairs and seen the table decorated and fresh flowers. He gave me a kiss and said. What special occasion is this?

There is talk in the church that you have a young girlfriend with a child. If you got a whore in the church with a baby can you stop your foolishness. You both going to hell together! You will go first and you better pray over your food it might be poison in it. Freddy, karma is real! Don't forget our first date you put a pill in my drink. Freddy eyes got big and spit out his food. I laughed and walked away and that became the end of them rumors. I got into my car and went to work. I had to go visit two church members while at work to check on them one was my cousin and she was having a baby. I was happy about that. I had to visit my mother she was in the hospital for her diabetes and the doctor said she can no longer work.

My mother had divorce my dad and remarried. Her husband was a good guy he stayed by her side. My life became overwhelmed with the job, church, husband, mother, and children. I battled depression all my life after Uncle Mike took my childhood from me. My sister in Christ Yvette came to the church to help take care of me. Yvette had helped everybody else family for so long. She neglected her children needs that led them out of control. We both were lost for words. We prayed to God that He would save us and our family. I became overwhelmed. I went on the alter one Sunday with my congregation and cried out. I told God to take this cup from me it is too hard to carry. I don't think it was wise of me to tell God

I didn't want to be the chosen one anymore. The days had become more intense for me as I kept pushing on this Christian journey.

I was at the hospital doing a twelve-hour shift. My sister Kenya was in the emergency room. I had not talked to her in a couple of months. I stopped and hugged her. She looked like she was sad to see me. I said Kenya are you ok? She said, yes! Kenya had brought our mother to the hospital. I just hate to see her like this. She has been the best mother anybody could ask for. When my real mother Wanda turned her back on me Mrs. Ruth took me in and always treated me special. I knew it was wrong for my mother to be sleeping with somebody husband. I hate dad! He could not get it together and treat Mother Ruth right. Now he is at my house driving us all crazy. He is talking about he wants Ruth back. We both start laughing saying, that's our dad.

I was having a week that was too much for me to handle. Every day I was hearing bad news. It was my own family that was battling sickness. I called Freddy. I told him to not wait up for me. I decided to go out with my nurse friends. My co-workers were drinking. I decided to order a drink. They said, Trina we thought you didn't drink. I don't, I am tonight. We all laughed. My deliverance was over. I opened the door and the demons came seven times stronger. I was too drunk to drive. My friends called an Uber. How can something so right go so wrong. Drunk laying in the bed with the enemy it became crazy. My husband was turned on by my drunk state of mind. We had sex like teenagers it was the best sex we have had in a long time. When we were finished he said, I am glad you are back Redbone. You need to start back drinking more often. I love the freak in you! I looked at him and seen he don't give a damn. I am drowning I can't swim! Only God can save me from my mess now.

Next day Freddy came home in a good mood. He decided to take me out something he had not did in a long time. Baby get on your best dress we going to dinner tonight. Freddy had me flowers and chocolate candy as he was talking and moving fast. Well baby I wanted to tell you how much I love you and the children. Trina you have always had my back. There is never going to be a woman like you. I had looked at Freddy and said thank you for your kind words. Freddy and I had picked up extra sex activities. My husband found out I wanted to be with women. Freddy signed us up for a sex club online. Freddy told me he gave me permission to be with other women. He would have to be there and watch. After months of fun my husband started joining me, that lead to our threesomes. Freddy had some attractive cousins that were very sexy and he wanted me to sleep with them. They were in the Swingers lifestyle. I will not be sleeping with you and your cousin that is just nasty Freddy. I am through with Swingers life. Freddy said I just want you and only you Mrs. Trina Love. The Swingers lifestyle had been over for the both of us for over a month. Freddy was playing "Keith Sweat make it last forever" in the car on the way to the restaurant. I almost thought this man was changing. I know he is up to something and that had me scared to death.

We got to the steakhouse and he parked the car and he opened my door. He held my hand while I stepped out the car. Freddy could be such a gentleman when he wanted something. We held hands he started kissing my hand. I felt for that moment I was the only one. I knew we had shared each other bodies with hundreds of people this year. I don't know how this thing got so deep now it is unstoppable. The waitress seated us at a booth. Freddy would not give me no room to breathe. This husband of mine was acting like a teenager this was not our first date out. Freddy what is wrong with you? Why you so happy? Baby things are really looking up for me in this church business. I decided to take out the person who made all this possible my true love Redbone. Freddy what are you talking about?

Baby we have got a big donation from the "Life Style organization" for the church. Freddy why in the hell would you mix sex and church together? You are out of order Pastor Freddy Love. No! Listen baby they are donating one hundred thousand dollars to use the church for a three-day conference. Freddy do you not know God is not having that in his church. You promised we were not living Swingers Life Style any more. Trina this is money for us and the family. Yes, it is that reminds me Freddy. I looked at our bank statements. I seen over two-thousand dollars' worth of baby items ordered. What are you up to Freddy?

My mother must of did that for the daycare and put it on the wrong account. I will get that fix. Yes, you better! If I find out you are sleeping around making babies that will be your last child you ever make or see! Freddy started sweating! I knew he was going to hang his self with more lies. Time will tell who he is taking care of. Who is worth this deal with the devil to cover up his financial debt? Married and in love living together for fifteen years. I can't shake this feeling of not being loved something is not right. I thought being married with four beautiful children would make me forget my past and not only that I'm the first lady at Apostle K & Prophet T Missionary Love Church the people are counting on me as the Prophet of the church. I am drunk on a Saturday night what will I say to the people with itching ears this Sunday

Chapter 10

UNFAITHFUL - LIAR LIAR PANTS ON FIRE

When I got home there were no children and the house was quiet. I went upstairs and heard my beautiful husband singing in the bathroom. I looked around and it looked like Freddy was going out. I opened the door to the bathroom and ask Freddy, where are you going? I got a meeting to attend about the church. Would you like to join me? He asks. No Freddy! I just did twelve hours at the hospital. Freddy got in the shower. I decided to get in with my husband to have a little fun. Freddy hit me on my butt and told me I had the best goodies in the state of Indiana. I wanted to say he did to. But that would be a lie! I still think about Chocolate Thunder and I took it out on my husband. Wow Trina! Why do you always give me good sex at the wrong time? Now I want to stay home with you. Freddy still left and I went to bed.

I woke up at 4:00am and Freddy was not home. I called his phone it went to voicemail. Where is my husband? I laid back down and went back to sleep. My alarm clock went off at 6:00am. I got up out of bed. My husband did not come home this is not like him. I got myself together for another long day at the hospital. Doctor Payne my Swingers' Club member decided to come on my floor. She shared my husband just helped deliver a baby. I looked at this hoe and said, Doctor Payne, I am not in the mood for your shit! I told you my husband and I no longer sleep with couples. We have left the Life Style game. Nurse Trina I am not here to upset you. If you don't trust my words go upstairs to the maternity ward yourself. I think that's what I will do. I became very nervous as I took the elevator to the 6th floor. Many things had started going through my brain. I got off the 6th floor. Who do I see sleep in the lobby? My husband and sister. Good morning Freddy! This adulterous looked like he seen a ghost. Good morning Trina! Why are you at the hospital with my sister? Kenya looked at me with puppy dog eyes.

Sister, I didn't know! I am sorry. What are you talking about? Freddy cut her sentence off. He said, I tell her Kenya. Somebody better explain why two people I love are sleeping next to each other in a hospital lobby. I just had a baby Trina! What? Yes! I tried to hide it. Me and Chloe just had a little girl together. No! This could not be true Freddy! You would not have slept with my niece! This is it you are no earthly good. Freddy this is the lowest you can go. I will have your things packed and all locks will be changed. Stay away from me and my children. Freddy started crying. He said, baby I didn't mean to hurt you again.

Next thing I know I took my stethoscope and chocked the hell out of this man. My sister was screaming! People were running to see what was going on. Security came and that didn't solve anything. I was not going to let Freddy get away this time. The police officers got there. It took two police to get me off Freddy. I was handcuffed while the nurses and doctors were seeing about Freddy. This must be the worst day of my life! I went to jail while at work. I feel so betrayed! Nobody loves me! God! Why do storms keep finding me?

People were looking from everywhere at the hospital. Doctor Payne walked up to me and shared she delivered the baby and she looks just like Freddy. Before I could hold back the tears. I spit in that whore face. The doctor laughed as she walked away saying enjoy jail Nurse Trina. I got in the police car with a struggle. The resistance didn't last long. The police beat my ass into the car. When the sheriff booked me, I was disoriented. I could feel my heart stop beating. No more pain, I collapse on the floor. I woke up in the nurse's office with infirmity that I could not explain. I was so angry. I can't replay this nightmare about my husband having sex with my niece that I raised as my daughter. How in the world did a forty-five-year-old man just become a father with an eighteen-year-old girl? Freddy Love will weep what he sows.

My attorney Mr. Blue he is a member of Pastor Jakes church. I called my attorney and told Mr. Blue what happened. He told me he would be right down to get me out. I am so happy I have people in the church that will see about me. I got out of jail with a five thousand dollars bond. The bad part about all this is I got suspended from my job. I needed to work to keep my mind at rest. Mr. Blue told me my husband posted the bond. I am glad to be free but I did not want anything from Freddy. I called a locksmith to meet me at home. Mr. Blue offer to take me home. I told him no. Mr. Blue I need time to think. Can you call me an Uber? I pulled up and my car was in the driveway. That let me know my husband been here. I hate this man but he always picks me up when I fall.

Freddy don't get it! He is my pain and suffering and I will not do it anymore. My locks were changed. I had a mover's company come and pack everything in the house that connected me to Freddy. I sent my husband a text before I changed my number. I told him all his clothes and furniture was put in storage. Freddy called me soon as I sent the text. Baby, I am so sorry! Freddy, I don't want to hear your shit! Your bed and everything you own has been sent to storage. Goodbye! I hung up my phone. I called the phone company changed all the numbers.

My mother Ruth was my hero she always helped with the children. My mother became quiet about Kenya and her family. My mother did not allow the baby over. Kenya told my mother she was sorry and she understand. Chloe was still going to church with the baby. I stopped going to church and giving my tithes. I started enjoying life. My husband said I was a whore. I just laughed and shared with him It takes one to know one Pastor Love! I had fun being single. I went back to work and everything was good. I started working in the blood bank of the hospital staying far out the way from Doctor Payne. I knew the doctor had power in the hospital but she was one of the leaders of the Swingers Club Associations. I spent more time with my children but the alcohol had been a must to cope with life issues. I loved this time without my husband. Freddy keeps coming around sitting in front of the house.

I had to call the police for him to leave the premises of the house. Freddy brought the damn police to my house saying he lives with me and we had a disagreement. I shared with the police my husband and I are separated. The police said, Mrs. Trina you must let your husband in his house. I said if I let this maniac in he will come out in a body bag! We have a no contact order. You need to do your research before you come knocking on doors to let a whore in that make babies with children! Freddy looked like he had been exposed. The police told him to contact his lawyer. If Freddy does this again he will go to jail for violation of the no contact order. This has been a long two months putting up with Freddy tricks. I decided to go back in the house and shower for bed.

(Dream in Hell)

I was screaming Freddy help me! Why is the fire so hot? Help me! I heard Freddy voice on the other side saying, Trina I am in hell I can't get to you please give me some water. It is so hot and no fun in hell. I am really paying for my sins. Baby, Jesus really sits on the throne next to God. I seen Heaven as I was going to Hell. Heaven is so beautiful!

God let me see it. Jesus said, you used my name but I did not know you. I missed the mark for heaven. I am so sorry baby how I treated you. I thought hell was not real. I'm here all day in the heat keeping heaven beautiful. God comes and pick up gold himself. He said if you make your bed in hell He come there to. Well that is true baby. Please get your life right. I don't want you here with me so many people that we grew up with is here this shit is crazy. I said, Freddy can you come back so we can talk about Chloe and the baby. Why did you do that to her and me? The next thing I seen was Freddy with shackled feet in the clouds. He screamed out loudly! I loved nobody but you Baby Redbone. Next thing I knew Freddy was being ordered to life in hell no return. Smoke surrounded me. I started choking, screaming, fighting, biting, and jumping my eyes opened.

To my surprise this was a dream taking place in my bed by myself. No Freddy insight. I was drenched with water my heart was beating. I knew I can't keep this feeling to myself anymore. Freddy must stop visiting me! Every night these dreams keep coming to me about Freddy. The dreams have become so real!

Chapter 11

Who is the Real Mrs. -To Death Do Us Part

Another day another dollar. I was running late for work. That dream had me up in the middle of the night. Freddy must get out of my life. He is always starting some type of controversy with me about the children, church, and family business. I got to deal with Freddy about the children. The rest of this mess the hell with. This fool starts drama between me and his mother every week about the children. Now that Freddy is out the house. I decided to go see my sister Kenya. When I got to her house I said a short prayer to God. Please let me stay calm when I see this baby amen. Kenya gave me a hug when I got in the house. Chloe was holding the baby. She said hi auntie. I spoke back. Chloe can I hold the baby? She said sure auntie. I looked at the baby and she looked so much like Chloe. She is beautiful just like you Chloe. I ask Chloe did the baby need anything? No! Auntie, she has everything.

Good I know my husband he going to take care of the children. It became real quiet until the baby started crying. Chloe got up. She asked for the baby back. I gave her the baby. Chloe said to the baby mommy know you hungry. She pulled out her breast and feed the baby. I asked what was the baby name? Her name is Shiloh. I like that name for the baby Chloe. Got to go to work. Just thought I would come by. Kenya thanks for letting me come to your house. You always been the peace maker of the family. Chloe, you and the baby be blessed.

When I got to work my supervisor had a note on my desk. I read the note: Nurse Trina, Doctor Payne has requested you to work with her on the labor and delivery unit for the next two weeks. Thank you for your flexibility at the hospital. This lady trying to make my job hard! I took my belongings and moved to the labor and delivery unit. I hope to stay out this doctor way. Soon as I got off the elevator Dr. Susan Payne was waiting on me. Trina, I need you to put your items up and come to my office we need to talk. I knew this was going to get crazy with this whore.

I went in Dr. Payne office and she said have a seat Trina. Look we have been friends for the last three years. I got you this job after our first threesome. You knew Freddy was a pimp he pimped you out for sexual favors and cocaine. Trina, I always took care of your needs and wants. My feelings for you are real. I have been devoted to you. Yes, you have Dr. Payne but we both married. Freddy was my pimp and gave me permission to be with other couples as he watched and took pictures. I am through with the Swingers Club my life with Freddy has ended.

My sexual activities are over. We have been on many swinger's trips together. I enjoyed partying with you. Freddy has done the unthinkable. I am moving on to a greater life without him. Trina, you can't just cut everybody off in the club. We count on you to be the life of the party. Freddy has talked with my husband and said you will be back. The judge has scheduled a meeting at our favorite hotel out in Fisher Indiana. You must come Trina everything will work out. Don't make this relationship difficult. Freddy still is in control of your sex life. This will be a Mardi Gras party. It will be six couples joining us. I will send you the hotel and suite number Wednesday afternoon.

I need you to be the head nurse this week Sheri is on vacation. Thanks Nurse Trina for all you do here at the hospital. Why didn't I transfer to another hospital when I beat the hell out of Freddy? My husband thinks he is still in control. Saturday will be the end of this swingers shit with him. Work is going great thanks to my girl Doctor Payne. I like being in charge but my team is working together. Doctor Payne has a lot of connection in the hospital. I will follow along with her demands to keep favor in the hospital. Work went fast and I am ready to go home. I stopped by the store and bought a prepaid phone. I got to call this crazy husband of mine. He can't get the new phone numbers. Freddy has been cut from my life. I hope my husband don't want to talk about moving back in.

When I called Freddy, he didn't answer. I decided to set up my voicemail so he could leave me a message when he called me back. I have had a long day. Mr. Freddy Love drama can wait until the morning. When I woke up for work my new To Go phone was blinking. I seen my soon to be ex-husband called me back. I decided to skip breakfast and listen to his message. I put the phone on speaker so I could get dress. Freddy voice was sounding sexy as he was telling me he misses us being a family. Trina, I hope to see you Saturday at the hotel. You should receive your costume in the mail Thursday. Redbone all you do is show up everything is taking care of. Why did Freddy mess our life up God! I will not go back to living a life of a broken whore. Heal me God do not let me perish!

Work went good all week. Friday came and Dr. Payne wanted us to go out together and have some drinks. I decided to take her up on her offer. We meet up in Fishers where all the party spots were. There were a lot of our colleagues hanging out enjoying life. This club has good food, drinks, and music. I do enjoy myself when I am out with Dr. Payne. Trina if we looked at our life through a glass bottle we both are whores. You can enjoy your life with Freddy and share him as he shares you. I have been entwined with you and your husband many of times. Mr. Payne keeps connecting with Freddy because he wants me happy and you keep me pleased. Freddy is just a cover up when I sleep with you. If I could have it my way I would just be with you Trina. My husband is my best friend but he knows I want to be with you.

I have chosen to keep my marriage open. I always loved women more. I have learned in a white-collar society you must do what is best for the family. My mouth was opened wide as I listened to Dr. Susan. Thanks for sharing this but I am a first lady my church is counting on me to bounce back. I am having a hard time dealing with what Freddy done to my niece that I raised. Freddy was a father figure why would he sleep with her and get her pregnant? Dr. Susan this is devastating to the whole community. We did not come from a high society culture. Poverty was so real in both our lives that we must disconnect from each other so healing can start. My family needs me they are all lost behind this lifestyle Freddy has created for our family.

Dr. Payne I am going home now because this was a long day. I will see you tomorrow Trina? Maybe, if not I will send somebody in my place. Dr. Susan I do care about you and always will. Freddy is my past and I will be divorcing him soon. I will never have sex with my husband again. I know I should go but after listen to the doctor I am going to sit this one party out and send my surprise guest. My life is trying to come together without Freddy. The children decided to do their own thing for the weekend. Time waits for nobody! My baby boy went over my mother's house for the weekend. This is Freddy weekend but he wants to go out and watch me have sex with the whole party. I need somebody to show him his pimp ass has played out!

Living for the weekends is my new hobby. A good movie and a glass of wine sounds like a winner. My cleaning, cooking, and laundry finished for the day. I Put my favorite movie on Rush Hour. I know the laughter will be good. After this movie bed, I go. I had falling asleep on the movie. Ring Ring Ring! I heard my house phone. When I picked up the phone and somebody was crying. I heard screaming on the other end of the phone. Trina, it went all wrong was all I heard and the phone went dead.

I turned on the television and breaking news was flashing before my eyes. There has been three people found dead at the Consulate Hotel. That is the same hotel the meeting was at. I checked my phone and knew Freddy was involved. I had fifty missed calls with so many unknown numbers. Let me check my voicemail. Mrs. Trina Love this is Detective Carlson can you call me at 317-444-2221. I tried to dial the number it was busy. The doorbell rang! I called the number again it started ringing while I opened the door. The police were at my door. I drop the phone with another voice on the line.

Are you Trina Love? The police ask. Yes, I am. Can you identify this Id of this person? That is my husband Pastor Freddy Love! The police told me my husband was dead from an overdose. I started screaming no! This can't be! We need you to come to the police station with us. Mrs. Love we have some questions to ask you. I answered the questions then I was released to go. I went home and tried to call some numbers back but still no answers. I need to go into the streets of Pigsville and find out what happened to my husband.

When I got to my mother-n-law house the block was hot. Police, media, and people everywhere. I had to turn around and go through the alley and park in the garage. I had keys to Capri house since I was a teenager. Her and Freddy would never want me homeless. I went in the house it was so crowded. I felt the love! People came from everywhere hugging me and crying. I was so heartbroken for my children. All seven of Freddy children where there. I went in the living room and hugged my step children. Freddy loved his children. Capri said, Trina I am glad you here we need to go upstairs and talk. We went to her room and sit down on her love seat. Capri started sharing what Freddy wanted if anything happened to him. She presented me a copy of his will. Freddy has requested no funeral and no viewing of his body. Freddy will be cremated after the autopsy.

Everything about Freddy will be handled later. Trina if you want to do a Passover at the church that would be nice. My son loved you and he did not want you to worry about anything. I will oversee everything. Capri reached out and hugged me we just cried on each other shoulders. Church I'm back! Watch out Chloe here I come! For better or worse, death do us part. Glad the wicked warlock is dead. Forgive me God my husband was Nightmare On Elm Street! I am free yes, I am free! My life was going pretty good but Chloe would not leave me along about this ugly child. The homicide detectives had come over my house to discuss Freddy death. It has been three months since my soulmate was found in a hotel with two other women. The autopsy came back that he had a heart attack. Mr. Ernest Kent had been the lead detective over the case. He did all the talking while the other detective just sat there. He was very handsome he didn't need to talk. I looked at Mr. Kent. I said, what do you have on my husband case? I came to ask you did you have any drug connections with your husband. No, detective Kent my husband did not sell drugs he was an honest man of the church. Freddy had given his life over to God. I wish he could of gave his penis over too but that is another story. We don't have anybody to target about the investigation. That has lead us back to you. We need to know more about you and Freddy separation. Detective Kent, that is none of your damn business. I will not be discussing that with you. You can leave my house now! Mrs. Trina Love did you know we found in the hotel room a digital scale, four hundred grams of marijuana, twenty-five blue tablets of controlled substance, ten grams of crack cocaine and your husband had three hundred dollars in his pocket. We will be back to talk more with you. We want to look over you and your husband's bank account. Mrs. Love enjoy your day because we will be back with a search warrant.

My pain is so deep that healing is hard for me this baby looks like my late husband. The toxicology report is taking forever. It is four months later and my husband death is still unsolved. Chole blames me for Freddy death. Chole had been wanting me to keep Freddy illegitimate child. The craziest thing about Chloe she thought her and the child would be in the obituary. I had to explain to her that was not legally established before Freddy death. What every Freddy did for her child is over. I tried to be nice to my niece about this ugly child. She keeps pushing me too far! I am the widow not her. The will can't be read for six months after Freddy death. I hope I can hold out from hurting her. Chloe still goes to the church sings in the choir. She prances around the church like she is in charge. I let her because I hold the money and she holds a dream. She told me since you poisoned my man you take care of his child. I told her I don't take care of unwanted children. I became evil after my husband died. Out of all of Freddy babies' mothers Chloe had performed the most in the Love family. This girl needs a reward for her mouth.

I know this stinky disrespectful child did not think I would take on her funny look alike child. I marched that ugly baby back to that fake, unholy, hypocritical church that my late husband was the pastor of and I am still First Lady. I went into the choir room and went to battle on Chloe my niece. It took the praise team and a police officer to stop me from killing her disrespectful want to be grown ass. Enough is enough Chole! I was the wife not you. I screamed out while I was taking away in hand cuffs. This dead husband of mine had damaged the whole church house before he died. The name of the church was even stupid just like my husband. He said he named it after us yea, right that nasty dog couldn't even spell the name Prophet T and Apostle K Missionary Love Church.

Chapter 12

Confession - Blame it on the Drugs and Alcohol

Here I am sitting in this jail cell for the last 90 days and I don't know how the hell I'm going home so I have decided to have a meeting with my covering pastor and his wife. My secrets and confessions will be shared today. I hope this truth that I share will free my soul from all my sins. I did not kill my husband. I still trying to figure out what whore at the church poisoned his black ass and left him to die in a 5-star hotel room. I am a little nervous meeting with my pastor. I hope my nurse come with my Xanax before my visit. I need something to take the shakes off, a cup of wine would do me good. It cost twenty-dollars for a cup of homemade wine in the Peppermint County Jail House.

I don't want to be drunk when I tell this hell of a story about my husband pimping his wife out for free. I thought I was coming home but Judge Payne decided to revoke my bond. He thinks I'm a threat to society. He can't believe I am a nurse. I kept looking at this judge and kept saying I know him from one of our church meetings Freddy would have. I got so angry about not going home I decided to stop thinking about who is this red neck judge. I stop daydreaming about the past when I heard my number called 250987 your medication is here. I was so glad to take my medication because this nasty prophet got some shit to tell that will blow the roof off my late husband's church. My Pastors Jake and Lynda Gray had always kept their word and that was hard to find in church people. I know they want the best for me.

When my pastors came to see me, we got a private room it is nice being clergy you get special privileges. Pastor Lynda started crying when she seen me but she gave me a hug and held me tight. Pastor Jake hugged me and sat right down then asked me where is your hair daughter? I laughed and said in the trash. I have started a new life. Pastor Jake did not laugh he gave me a frown and quickly grabbed my hand and they started praying.

Pastor Jake can pray heaven down to touch anybody on earth. God, I hope you are listen because I need away out and quick. I started crying and pastor Lynda cried with me saying Trina it is alright it is nothing too hard for God to do. I looked at both my loving pastors saying you don't understand this may be dangerous. I am a whore and my dead husband was my pimp. I sold my soul to the devil and don't know how to get back to Christ. Pastor Jake said no daughter you are a wonderful person we are forgiving for all our sins. Trina God will forgive you for fighting people remember when they came to kill Jesus and the disciples were fighting to protect him. They cut a man ear off then Jesus put it back on.

God understand this young lady was sleeping with your husband and made a baby. I am not talking about my charges of why I am in here. I had to tell him it is bigger than Chloe. That did not unfold until months before Freddy's murder. Pastor Jake I hope you can handle what I need to share. I have lived on Nightmare on Elm St. with Freddy Krueger. Me and other teenagers had falling prey to this man. Pastor Lynda laughed and her husband chuckled saying this is not a movie Trina I don't think you can compare your life to a psychopath that went around killing people. Well you be the judge of that. I am just going to tell you about the last three years that I lived on drugs and alcohol after my deliverance and church hurt.

They looked at me and said Trina you been a first lady for five years at your own church honey. I screamed and hit the table! No, I have taken my medication for today and I am trying to confess my sins please listen! Ok calm down, we are here for you. Pastor Lynda you not ready for this. I don't know how to start off. I want to keep the church and the daycare open. My mother was a whore and my father was her pimp now I have followed the same pattern. I did not know my parents they gave me away to a family member. My heart weights heavy because of the same thing that hurts me. Abandonment! Now look at my children they have experience my pain in its worst form.

Pastor Jake I loved my husband he was my everything but he never could be faithful to me. I decided to join my husband whoredom. I did not know it would lead me to losing my career and children. Why did you go back to sin? Lynda asked. Because the life of a Christian became too hard for me to live. I felt like I was the only one living right. The fight for salvation should had been easy Jesus had already paid the price. Pastor Jake I loved having both worlds but the church world was fake because people are so vulnerable. Freddy knew that would be a good place to use others. I know God is real and I hear him but I decided to be with the devil.

My husband gave me permission to have sex with multiple people at the same time. I felt in my heart it was ok to join others in sex because it was approved by my husband. It was not cheating. Freddy loved me I thought. When I found out about the others he had been with and made children with them. I knew he hated me. Freddy shared me with the whole world pimped me out. All I was worth were drugs for him and party life for me. Freddy wanted everybody to have a piece of me even some of his family members. Pastor Jake said Trina Freddy was a sick man and he was the leader of the household. You and your family became sick with him but you must start over ask for forgiveness and sin no more, God loves you.

Freddy is dead he did not get a second chance he died in his sins with 2 women in the bed with him over dosed on drugs. Tears just started falling down my face! Pastor Jake I am a numb woman. I don't think I ever knew how to love. My heart is so broken. I felt like there was never a breakthrough for me. I lived a Christian life for five years out of the thirty-five and it was the best feeling in my life. The hardest thing for me was trying to accomplish living holy but it didn't happen on my time. Freddy refused to believe in the true living God he told me it was a job and he had mastered Christian life. I let God down but it is strange how I feel God presents here in jail. Trina, me and pastor will be praying for you this is a lot to take in. God covers a multitude of sins just stay strong and we will work on your request for the church and daycare.

Legal problems for Apostle K & Prophet T Missionary Love Church has started. Pastor I need a legal representative to change the church name. Pastor Jake said that will be a good ideal Trina we can handle that for you. Pastor I still would like you and Lynda to stay the covering while Pastor Kent Bush and his wife Robin stay the leaders. They have run the church for the last three years while me and Freddy were serving the devil put them on salary pay. I will be signing all my businesses to you. Freddy mother and aunt had handled the church prayer and finances for the last five years. I need that to stop but make sure she and her sister are taken care of they really have been good to me.

Now back to my confession. I am bisexual. I told Freddy this three years ago when I went back to drinking, smoking cigarettes, and marijuana. I know as a Christian not to act out on my feelings but I was lusting for a woman and shared it to Freddy. I know it is wrong about my thoughts for wanting to be with a woman. I was no longer happy with Freddy. I assured my husband I had never stepped out of our marriage. Freddy said it was good I shared that and he would make sure I never felt like this again. Pastor Jake looked at me and said this could not be daughter.

Sorry pastor I cut my hair off and went bald because I will play the man roll. I am the more dominant one in all my relationships. I recall most the time at the parties I didn't know what was going on when the sex started it became outer body experiences. I am sharing this because I did not poison my husband. I am glad he is dead. I love Chloe as my own child. She was brained washed by Freddy just like me as a child. The other five young women he dated in the church. I found out that Freddy had sexual desires for Chloe at my house and Chloe told my twins and they confronted Freddy that lead into a physical fight. All the girls held this a secret until Chloe came up pregnant. When everything in my life started falling apart and the girls went to stay with their dad. I went back to drinking and my healing and deliverance went out the window from that day on. I have been a disappointment to the church. To tell the truth all this is Freddy fought he brought other people into our bedroom.

Pastor the next day Freddy brought one of the women from the church over and had us drinking then the woman started feeling on me. I looked at Freddy and he said it is ok. I told you I would take care of you. The strange thing is Freddy joined in and he was very familiar with this woman pleasures. I found out this was the lady Octavia that sang in the choir that he was seen out number of times with her and her baby. He didn't take me and his family out. Pastor Jake had his mouth opened and his wife was crying. The good part about all of this is Freddy stopped beating on me after that night. What the Hell you mean beating on you Trina? Pastor Jake blurted out. The guard came over to the table and told us to lower our voices. I told you when he blacked your eye we would not tolerate no kind of abuse why did you let him keep hurting you?

Because he did not hurt me too much. Please pastor Jake let me tell you the most important part of this confession. Nothing could be as bad as this right here Trina your husband was a monster! Lynda screamed shut up Jake! Let Trina talk. I knew this confession could shake up the dead and Freddy is rolling over in his urn. Funny just a thought. Lynda spoke out saying please finish what you are saying Trina. We are here for you and she grabbed my hand as she was talking. Jake and I are sorry Freddy treated you badly. We are not here to call people names or judge. My brain was all over the place. I had to think about where I left off at before pastor said Freddy was a monster. Freddy lead me to a whole new world of entertainment called "The Lifestyle".

Pastor are you familiar with swingers that what Mr. and Mrs. Freddy Love were doing for the last three years. Are you telling me your husband pimped his own wife out to the whoredom world? Yes, I believe our commitment to the weekend partying has caused my heartache in jail with no bond. We were with people in high places. I found out that Freddy had been sexually touching my niece Chloe for years. When she turned eighteen he started having sex with her and got her pregnant. My whole world ended and that is when me and Freddy got into that big fight. I tried to kill him but instead the police came and sent me to jail. All the ass beatings he gave me for over twenty damn years!

Now I am known as the abuser this shit is funny. Pastor the church thought we had been on vacation but I was in jail and Freddy was recovering from his injuries. Freddy has been doing cocaine and other drugs for years hiding them through the pulpit. This Sexual Life Style got out of hand when Freddy wanted me to sleep with more church members and a few of his family members. I had to put a stop to this foolishness we got to the point we had lost all morals, respect, and trust for one another. Freddy would set up the dates because that is one of the rules when you have agreed to the Life Style society. Freddy was in the hotel with who killed him this shows he was still cheating after I had given myself totally to him and the devil. I am so hurt I want to die.

Pastor Jake said, Trina this society you have joined is dangerous I don't think you can just stop being a whore. Lynda shouted out please Jake let's not talk to Trina like this is serious. I know Pastor Jake because when I left Freddy the judge put a non-contact order in place. Freddy thought it was a joke and wanted me to still have sex with him. Freddy gave my number out to more swingers and they were calling me asking me to party that breaks all rules. All sexual meetings were set up by the husband. I would not have nothing to do with Freddy Love. I told him he was sick and needed help. He just laughed and called me a whore and prostitute if he can't have me nobody will. Pastor Lynda was crying and pastor Jake did the talking. I think this is going to be overwhelming to hear more of this confession! Are you ok Pastor Lynda?

Pastor Jake answered before his wife could open her mouth. Your soul is corrupted my daughter this is not normal this is very out of human character. But There is a Way Out through Christ Jesus so the big question is can you tell us how many people have you slept with? We need to start the healing process with breaking every soul tie you have linked yourself to. I don't know pastor we went out almost every Friday and Saturday and we went on trips and nude camps. In the last three years so I would say hundreds to thousands I really can't tell you I did a lot of outer body experiences.

Freddy would have to show me by pictures or tell me about it. Freddy would get so angry. I did not remember what was going on with our sex life at the meetings. I did not care about the sex I was doing that for Freddy. I felt like a famous person so many wealthy people requested me and we had plenty of alcohol, drugs, sex toys and whatever you wanted. Pastor Jakes said we going to stop this session and get you a Christian Therapist but we got to work on getting you out of jail. I don't understand Trina why you don't have a bond. We told the judge and prosecutors you are a well-known pastor on the west side community plus a nurse at a massive hospital.

Pastor do you know Judge Payne? I talked to him when you went to court in April. We came to your court date but we were a little late. I missed you and the prosecutor said they had already arrested you and took you to the back. Pastor said, Trina me and Lynda thought it was strange that the judge was talking like he knew you. He had sentence you without a trial. Pastor I just put my thinking cap on I know where I know Judge Payne from. He is part of Life Style and me and Freddy were involved with his wife. But why is he holding me in a jail cell I am not trying to expose him. The judge wife is a doctor at the hospital. I worked for her but I had to resign because I still can't get a new bond why would he say I am a threat to society.

This is not adding up. What do my swingers life style do with Judge Payne holding me in jail revoking my bond? Pastor Jake if I don't get out of here I am going to sing like a birdy and we all be in a bird cage. Pastor Lynda started singing the blood of Jesus has never lost its powers and she started talking in tongues this had got to deep and the spiritual warfare was on!! God please get me out of here I need you. I started saying we had church at the end of the visit my situation looks like the end for my life but my faith is everlasting and I'm coming out of HELL. I guess it is time to find out who killed my husband and what do "Swingers Life Style" got to do with me held up in the Peppermint County Jail system.

Printed in the United States
By Bookmasters